Ted Rules the World

frank cottrell boyce

Illustrated by
Cate James

Barrington  Stoke

First published in 2022 in Great Britain by
Barrington Stoke Ltd
18 Walker Street, Edinburgh, EH3 7LP

www.barringtonstoke.co.uk

This story was first published in a different form in
The Birthday Book (Random House Children's Books, 2008)

This 4u2read edition based on *Ted Rules the World*
(Barrington Stoke, 2015)

Text © 2015 & 2022 Frank Cottrell Boyce
Cover Illustrations © 2008 Chris Riddell
Internal Illustrations © 2015 Cate James

A CIP catalogue record for this book is available
from the British Library upon request

ISBN: 978-1-80090-103-2

Printed by Hussar Books, Poland

To Héloïse,
who will one day rule the world

Contents

Chapter 1

A New Prime Minister

I love it when you wake up early on your birthday. You can lie there and think about all the excellent new stuff that is coming your way.

When I woke up on my birthday, my mum and dad were already downstairs.

That must be a monster surprise they're getting ready down there, I thought. *It's only half past six. It has to be a quad bike.*

I stayed in bed a bit longer. I didn't want to mess up their big moment. In the end, I just couldn't wait. I ran down the stairs.

"Hi, Mum. Hi, Dad," I said.

There wasn't a quad bike. Or a new PlayStation. Or an iPhone in a smart new box. My mum and dad were in fact asleep on the sofa.

"Hi, Mum. Hi, Dad," I said again, a bit louder this time.

Mum opened one eye. "Oh. Ted," she said. "Hi. Turn the telly off, will you?"

Dad opened both eyes. "Oh. Ted," he said. "I wanted to say something to you ..."

"Was it happy birthday?" I asked.

"No. It'll come back to me." And he went off to sleep again.

I looked around the room for big and expensive presents hidden somewhere.

Nothing. I turned the telly off and that woke Dad up again.

"It's over," he said. "We've got a new Prime Minister. Goodnight."

Chapter 2
Evil Owen

Mum and Dad had stayed up all night to watch the election results and had totally forgotten my birthday. If I was the new Prime Minister, I'd pass a law against that right away.

I'd also pass a law against people who throw other people's bags off the back of the school bus. People like Evil Owen.

On the morning of my birthday, Evil Owen sat across from me on the bus to school and laughed at my hair for three stops.

"Look at his hair," Evil Owen said. "It's hilarious."

"It's not hilarious," I said. "It's red."

"Exactly," he said. "Red with a hint of hilarious."

"Leave him alone," my friend Benedict said. "It's his birthday."

"Oh, is it?" said Owen. "Then it's time for a surprise."

And he grabbed my bag, opened the window at the back of the bus and dropped the bag out of it.

I had to get off at the next stop and walk half a mile back up the High Street to find it again. On my birthday.

If I was Prime Minister and stuff like that was going on in my country, I wouldn't sleep at night.

Chapter 3
Hula Hoops

At birthday parties when I was little, my favourite thing was always Hula Hoops. Not the hula hoops that you hula with – the crisps.

I don't know what it is about Hula Hoops. I think it's because you can put one on the end of each finger and pretend you're eating your fingers. Or something.

Anyway, I wasn't sure that Mum and Dad would come up with birthday Hula Hoops this year. So, on the way home from school, I stopped off at the new supermarket at the end of our road. It's called "NextDoor". I got a massive party pack of Hula Hoops and some Happy Birthday paper cups for myself.

"Somebody's birthday today?" the nice lady on the till asked. Perhaps she was the great grand-daughter of Sherlock Holmes.

"Yes," I said. "It's mine."

I was going to tell her about how my parents had slept the whole day, but she smiled at me. "Happy birthday!" she said. "Here's a present for you – our new loyalty card. There you go." And she gave me a little purple plastic card. "Every time you buy anything here, we'll put points on that card for you. And points mean prizes."

I wasn't sure.

"I'm not sure," I said.

"You can have this mammoth pack of Premier League collector's cards for free," she

said. "As a welcome present, and because it's your birthday. What football team do you support?"

I explained that because of my family I supported the historic but basically rubbish team of Stockport County.

"Oh," the nice lady said. "Well, I'm sure you're a proper fan."

When I got home, there was a big HAPPY BIRTHDAY poster stuck to the door and a table full of food. There was even a bowl of Hula Hoops so big you could swim in it.

Plus I got an amazing bike. With about a million gears. And my cousins came round and we had a massive on-bike water fight.

So Mum and Dad had got their act together just in time and given me a brilliant birthday.

While we cleared up, we watched the new Prime Minister on TV. When she said that she supported Stockport County too, we thought it was surprising but not weird. Things didn't get properly weird for another week.

Chapter 4

Soup in Tins

A few days later I stopped off at NextDoor again.

This time there was a different nice woman, and she was standing by the fruit and veg with a clipboard.

"Could you answer a few questions for our survey?" she said.

She asked me my name and how I got to the shop and whether I liked soup in tins more than soup in boxes. Then she smiled at me.

"And do you think it would be a good idea
if all children were made to walk to school,
just one day a week?" she asked. "It would
help save the planet, make roads less busy and
raise fitness levels. What do you think?"

"Sure," I said. "But some people in our school have to travel quite far. Maybe you could say everyone who lives within a mile of the school has to walk."

"Great. I'll put that down," she said.

I spotted that party packs of Hula Hoops were on a 2-for-1 offer. But I wasn't interested in Hula Hoops any more. Now what I wanted was some cheesy breadsticks.

That night, on the news, the new Prime Minister launched a new plan to make every child walk to school one day every week.

"But what about children who live miles away from school?" the TV presenter said.

The Prime Minister smiled. "My plan is only for children who live within a mile of the school," she said.

"Well," the TV presenter said, "it sounds like a Prime Minister has had a good idea at last."

"Thank you," the Prime Minister said. "I'm going to do it myself. On Fridays I shall walk from Downing Street to Parliament. It should help me keep slim."

The presenter said something polite about how the Prime Minister wasn't fat.

And this is where it gets a bit weird. Because the Prime Minister smiled again. "Not yet," she said. "But I've been really laying into the cheesy breadsticks of late."

And as she said this last bit, I swear she looked right at me. From the telly. And winked. At me.

Chapter 5

A Law that Works

That Friday was the first ever Walk to School day. Evil Owen took my bag and threw it. But we were no longer on a moving bus, so all I had to do was stop and pick it up. At last a government had passed a law that worked.

That was the day Mum asked me to pick up some carrots and potatoes on the way home from school. "If you do it," she said, "you'll get extra points on your loyalty card."

Benedict came with me and I showed him the card.

"That's a terrible photo," he said.

"I don't remember them taking a photo of me," I said. "And how come the card has my name printed on it? They didn't even ask me my name." How weird was that?

Benedict said it wasn't weird at all. "Supermarkets know everything about you," he said. "I bet they even know we're having this conversation. They know all about us because of social media."

There was a massive line of people at the checkout, but the supervisor came up to me.

"Mustn't keep our loyal customers waiting," she whispered. "Till 7 is open for you."

I slipped out of the line and got to Till 7 just as the nice woman from the first night was sitting down behind the scanner.

"Hello." She smiled. "And how are things at Stockport County?"

"We need a defender who can pass the ball as well as stopping it," I told her.

"I see," she said.

And she checked out my vegetables and yawned. "Don't you think it would be better if the weekends started on Fridays?" she said.

"No," I said. "It would be better if they went on until Monday."

"Oh." She nodded. "Maybe you're right. No Hula Hoops tonight then?"

"No," I said. "But I'll take a packet of Premier League collector's cards, please."

"Sold out, I'm afraid."

Chapter 6

Stockport County

That evening the Prime Minister was on TV again with another new plan. Everyone would get Mondays off.

"It will help save the planet and improve the work-life balance," the Prime Minister said. "We all know that work will always fill the time you give it, so why not just give it less time?"

It was a massively popular move.

"You must be very happy, Prime Minister," the TV presenter said.

"I'd be happier," she said – and she looked right at me as she said it – "if Stockport County had a defender who could pass the ball instead of just blocking it."

That was when I knew for sure. That was when the weirdness made sense. It was all clear now.

The woman at the till was working for the Prime Minister.

The Prime Minister wanted my advice.

In fact, she wanted me to run the country.

I told Benedict this.

"Why would the Prime Minister want you to run the country?" he said.

"Well, because I'm really clever," I said. "I came second in the Maths test, remember, and I got a star for my History story. Why

wouldn't she want me to help her run the country?"

"I think," Benedict said, "that you've eaten so many Hula Hoops you've gone doolally."

"I'll show you," I said.

We stopped off at NextDoor. They still didn't have any Premier League collector's cards. I went up to the nice woman at the till.

"Still no Premier League collector's cards, I see," I said. "Someone should do something about that. Children can't focus on their school work. And it's putting them at risk. The fewer cards there are, the more those cards are worth. Which means bullies will beat you up to get your cards off you."

"I'll see what I can do." And the nice woman smiled.

Benedict came back to ours for tea. I put on *Newsround*. There she was – my own little Prime Minister. Here is what she was saying.

"The Premier League collector's cards teach children how buying and selling work. When there aren't many cards, the cards are worth more. But things have reached crisis point and we are hearing that children have been beaten up for some cards. I intend to bring back order to our playgrounds and so I will be giving out free Premier League cards in all our playgrounds in the next few days."

Benedict looked at me. "You," he said, "are the Leader."

Chapter 7

Genius

We were waiting in line for our free Premier League cards the next day.

"I just can't work out why it's you," Benedict said.

"Think about it," I said. "They've been doing tests on us since we were little – SATs tests, CATs tests, you name it. They know everything about us. They just put all the facts together, stuck them in a computer, ran a test and I came out top."

"I can't see that," Benedict said. "I mean, you're not even top of our class, never mind of the world."

"OK," I said. "I'm not top in exams, just top as in a top guy. Top person."

"I don't think so," Benedict said. "If you were, you'd be making cool things happen."

"How do you mean?" I asked.

Benedict held up his hands. "Well, come on, you're in control of the country and all you've done is get us a few extra Premier League cards. You could really improve people's lives."

Of course Benedict was right. The Prime Minister had asked for my help. Why? Because I'm a genius. Because I could save the world. But how?

I lay awake all night thinking about how I could stop global warming, war, car crashes,

hunger and make Stockport County winners again.

On the way to school I saw litter in the streets, petrol fumes in the air, babies crying in buggies. I felt as if all that was my fault. I needed to make things change.

Benedict met me at the school gates. "I tell you what I found on YouTube," he said. "A film of a snake swallowing an antelope. Why don't they put stuff like that on the news and not stories about murders and wars? Why don't you pass a law about that?"

"Benedict," I said, "shut up. And carry my bag. It's too heavy and I can't think."

Benedict looked hard at me. "You've changed, Ted McKillop."

"Of course I've changed," I said. "I'm trying to save the planet."

At lunchtime I sent Benedict to get me some hot food while I went and sat on an empty table so I could do some thinking.

From time to time I looked up at all the other kids. They were laughing and shoving each other and eating. So chilled. That's because they're not geniuses. They don't have to save the world.

Benedict brought me a pasta bake, an apple and some Vimto.

"The apple is for energy and the Vimto will wake up your brain," he said. "The pasta is ... well, it's horrible. You couldn't pass a law about school dinners, could you? Or – shall I tell you my idea? It's a way to end wars."

"A way to end wars?" That sounded good. "Yeah. Go on."

"Well, what you could do is ... Instead of sending planes to bomb people and innocent children ... What if each country got its top scientists to bring back a dinosaur?"

"Bring back a dinosaur?" I said.

Benedict nodded. "From dinosaur DNA. Any dinosaur you like and then we wouldn't need to send rockets and bombers. Each country could just send their dinosaurs to fight each other. No one gets hurt. Except the dinosaurs. And you could stop spending trillions of dollars, because you would make money because everyone would want to watch it. On TV. I mean, say it was a T. Rex versus a Diplodocus, you'd want to watch that, wouldn't you? Who wouldn't?"

"Benedict," I said, "you don't understand."

"I think the Diplodocus would probably win because of its tail," Benedict went on. "All it would need to do—"

"Sssh," I said. I was looking at the apple he'd got me. It had a label that said it was from South Africa.

I thought about all the food that flew around the world. Sometimes food from countries where people were starving came all the way to our country for rich people to eat. And if it was broccoli or something, I bet people wouldn't even eat it.

I could feel my idea coming. Something about leaving food where it was. You'd stop all the pollution from the planes. People in poor countries would have food. And there'd be less waste – broccoli, for example – in this country. Genius.

I was beginning to understand why the Prime Minister had picked me.

"What are you smiling at?" It was Evil Owen who said this. He was looking right at me.

I couldn't say it, could I? "I may have just solved the problem of hunger and global warming in one go." No, I couldn't.

So I said, "I'm not sure. I think the label must have fallen off my apple."

Evil Owen growled, picked up my bag and lobbed it across the dining hall.

It hit our head of year, Mr Mercer, smack in the face. Mr Mercer gave me a detention.

"But, sir ..." I wanted to explain that:

1. it wasn't me, and

2. I had to save the world and so I was too busy to have detention.

But Mr Mercer wouldn't listen. "It's your bag," he said. "It hit me. You're in trouble."

"But Owen threw it, not me," I said.

"Then you shouldn't let him throw it," Mr Mercer said. "It's your bag."

Chapter 8
Nothing Special

By the time I got out of school, there were massive queues in NextDoor.

A nice voice came over the sound system.

"Would Ted McKillop please report to the information desk?" the nice voice said. "That's Ted McKillop to the information desk, please."

When I got there, the nice woman from the till was waiting for me.

"We can't have you waiting at the till like our other customers." She smiled. "How are you today?"

"I feel OK for a redhead," I said. "People with red hair are always getting into trouble. We're always getting the blame for stuff just because it's easy to spot us. There should be a law that says if a redhead gets blamed for something, they probably didn't do it."

I know I should have told her my brilliant idea for ending poverty and global warming in one go. But I was too upset about getting the detention. It wasn't fair. It was Evil Owen that threw my bag at Mr Mercer, not me.

My Prime Minister was on the news two days later telling us about the Redheads Innocence Act.

If the police arrested any redhead, they had to set them free again unless the police had photos that proved they had done the crime. If a redhead went to court, he had two lawyers not just one like anyone else.

Not everyone thought it was a good law. Criminals started to dye their hair red so they'd have a better chance of getting away with it. People from Africa and China and South America – in fact, most people in the world – were annoyed because they hardly ever have red hair. There were blond riots in Manchester and Glasgow. Bald people went on strike in Wales.

I felt I was a bit to blame for all this. So I didn't go to NextDoor for a week or so. Then a letter came in the post. It said:

N

Great news! We have selected

your loyalty card from millions

of others. You have won a ride in

our special NextDoor helicopter!

It will collect you from your back

garden any minute now!

Any minute now? I looked out of the kitchen window. I couldn't see a helicopter. I carried on reading the letter. It said:

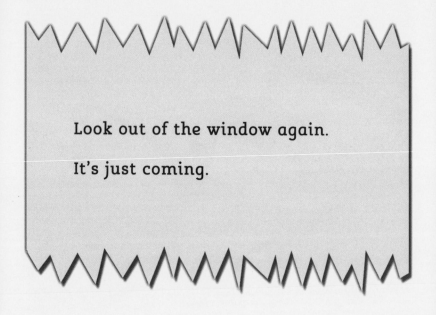

Look out of the window again.

It's just coming.

And there was a helicopter. It jerked as it dropped down towards the garden, churning up grass clippings and compost. Dad came running downstairs.

"Who is that maniac?" he yelled. "Look at what he's doing to my apple trees!"

The apple trees were thrashing about like goths in a mosh pit. A ladder dropped down from the cockpit.

"Got to go, Dad," I said. "See you later."

"You're not getting in there!" he yelled. "What have I told you about taking lifts from strangers?"

But it wasn't a stranger. It was the nice lady from the till in NextDoor.

"Sorry about the helicopter," she said. "But the noise is good. No one can hear us talk. This is a secret talk."

"Right," I said.

"You know that we've been using you as a kind of secret adviser," the lady said. "You've been brilliant so far but now you've let us down."

"I know," I said. "I'm sorry. I was upset. I can explain."

She held up her hand. "It's not your fault. It's ours. We never asked you. It was our idea. Not yours. Have you worked out why we chose you?"

"Because I'm a genius?" I said. "I came second in my Maths test and third in History and—"

"No," the nice lady from the till said. "We chose you because you were average. We looked at all the SATs scores, CATs scores, school exams, shopping habits and TV habits. You are the most average boy in the country. We thought that anything you like, most people would like too. Because you are like most people. There's nothing special about you. Or we thought there was nothing special about you. But we didn't know about your hair."

She leaned closer. "You see, on CCTV footage your hair looks like normal hair," she said. "But, in fact, there's nothing normal about it. It's fantastic. And a bit hilarious. It's not average. I guess the lesson for us is that no one is average. Everyone is special. We'll try to remember that in future. In the meantime, this helicopter ride is your thank-you present ..."

"Oh, thanks," I said.

"And it's also to help you remember," she said. "If you ever say a word about this to anyone, a squad of commandos in a helicopter like this one will snatch you and fly you out of the country. You will live out the rest of your days in a secret hide-out with no TV and only goats for friends. You have to remember that."

"Oh. Right," I said. "Well. I won't forget."

"Good," the lady from the till said. And that was the end of our secret talk.

Chapter 9

Back to Normal?

So that was it.

I went back to being Ted McKillop, the most average boy in Britain.

Everything was just the same except the weekend still went on until Monday and we had to walk to school on Fridays. People looked a bit happier. And that was down to me. Life went back to normal.

After that, the only exciting thing that happened was Benedict's birthday. He got a bike too, and we had another massive bike and water fight. It was only afterwards, when we were eating pizza, that I saw the NextDoor loyalty card on the shelf.

"After this, do you fancy a quick go on the PlayStation?" I said.

"No, I really want to watch the news tonight," Benedict said.

"The news? On your birthday? Why?"

"I just do."

So we watched the news. The lead story was "Snake Swallows Antelope Whole".

"Cool," said Benedict.

And in my memory, I heard him go on. "Tell you what I found on YouTube ... blah blah blah ... a snake swallowing an antelope whole ... blah blah blah ... put stuff like that on the news?"

I smiled. "OK, that's enough news," I said.
"Let's get on the PlayStation."

Our books are tested
for children and young people by
children and young people.

Thanks to everyone who consulted on
a manuscript for their time and effort in
helping us to make our books better
for our readers.